DREAM WEAVERS

CHAOS OF THE FUN FIEND

To my Dream Team – Angelique, Helena and Maria
– AS

To Olivia, my little dreamer
– FB

LITTLE TIGER
An imprint of Little Tiger Press Limited
1 Coda Studios, 189 Munster Road, London SW6 6AW

Imported into the EEA by Penguin Random House Ireland,
Morrison Chambers, 32 Nassau Street, Dublin D02 YH68

A paperback original
First published in Great Britain in 2024

ISBN: 978-1-78895-646-8

A CIP catalogue record for this book is available from the British Library.

Printed and bound in the UK.

The Forest Stewardship Council® (FSC) is a global, not-for-profit organization
dedicated to the promotion of responsible forest management worldwide. FSC® defines
standards based on agreed principles for responsible forest stewardship that are supported
by environmental, social, and economic stakeholders. To learn more, visit www.fsc.org

10 9 8 7 6 5 4 3 2 1

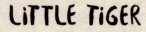

LiTTLE TiGER

LONDON

DREAM WEAVERS

CHAOS OF THE FUN FIEND

ANNABELLE SAMI

ILLUSTRATED BY
FORREST BURDETT

CHAPTER ONE
A DREAM HOLIDAY

"On your marks ... get set ... go!"

I press down on the airhorn with all my might and it honks loudly.

The competitors sprint across a long racetrack that I weaved across my dreambase and I grip the stopwatch in my hand tightly. The racers – an ostrich, a kangaroo, a cheetah, an alligator and a monkey – are almost at the finish line when...

"Hey!" I shout, before blowing a whistle. "That's a foul!"

The cheetah had curled its tail around the

kangaroo's leg to trip it up so they could win the race! I really should have seen that coming.

"I demand a rematch!" the monkey announces.

"And the cheetah should be disqualified!" croaks the alligator.

I sigh and wave my hands in circles as if I'm washing a window, making the animals and the track fizzle into thin air.

At the start of this year, the thought of holding an Olympic Games for talking animals would have been one, impossible and two, bonkers. But that was before I met Neena. She joined our class this term, having moved from Pakistan, and once she knew she could trust me, she told me that I'm a Dreamweaver just like her!

Now we have adventures in our dreams almost every night. It's not all silly races, though – there has been the odd run-in with jinn, spirits like scary fairies and a hangry wolf, but we've managed to control them.

There's also the small problem of Neena's uncle – a Darkweaver known as the Bhoot, who has an evil plan to try to merge the spirit and human worlds together… Something we *absolutely* cannot let happen.

That's why I'm holding the Olympics here in my dreambase, a clifftop I call Titotown. I need to practise my dreamweaving skills so I'm ready for whatever comes next. Be it fairy, beast or Darkweaver.

OK … *and* because it's fun.

I'm about to try a two-hundred-metre race when a voice floats towards me on the breeze… It's calling my name.

Titoooo… Titooooo!

I breathe in sharply and then *BAM*.

I'm lying flat on my face on the floor of Neena's bedroom, and she's poking me in the arm. "Tito, wake up! Your mama's going to be here soon to pick us up."

I wipe the drool from the corner of my mouth and groan. "How long was I asleep?" I ask shyly.

"Only about five minutes," Neena replies. "Were you doing the Titotown Olympics again? What event was it this time?"

"Hundred-metre sprint," I yawn. "But the cheetah cheated."

Nina giggles. "You created a whole race in just a nap? That's amazing, Tito!"

I perk up at the compliment. "My dreamweaving skills are getting stronger, aren't they? It wasn't that long ago I couldn't even dreamweave a pizza without it being made of cardboard." Remembering the cheesy-cardboard monstrosity, I heave myself up off the floor.

It's 5 p.m. on a Friday and pitch-black outside – winter is here. Today was our final day of school before the holidays and it was very tiring. I'd drifted off while Neena was still talking to me.

"What were you saying before I fell asleep?" I yawn again.

"I was asking what kind of present to bring your nan and grandad," Neena reminds me. "Do they prefer biscuits or chocolate?"

"Ummmm, honestly, both."

"Chocolate biscuits it is, then." Neena nods.

This holiday is going to be *extra* special because Neena is coming with my family to my nan and grandad's house!

Since we got home from school, she's been packing her clothes into a small purple suitcase while I tell her about Everwood – the seaside town where my grandparents live. Well, I *was* telling her before my nap.

"Nan and Grandad are basically kids at heart – that's what Mum always says," I explain. "We're going to have so much fun!"

"Tell me about the prank your grandad does again," Neena says, folding up a top. "The one with the coin."

I start laughing before I even begin telling the story. "He pretends he's accidentally swallowed a penny then he makes you pull his finger and it drops out of his trouser leg!"

Neena joins me laughing.

"And Nan is the best at made-up
imagination games, like zookeepers or
adventurers. Plus there's a fairground and an
arcade that are even open in winter. And a
Sea Life centre with starfish you can touch!"

"Oh my gosh, I can't *wait*!" Neena squeals.

Ameena, Neena's mum, appears in the
doorway holding a steaming cup of chai.
She smiles at us both. Neena's mum is
a Soothsayer – someone in touch with
the spirit world. She is a Starreader, and

sometimes I swear I can see the stars sparkling in her kind green eyes.

"Did you find everything I left you to pack, darling? Tito's mama is downstairs waiting."

Since we have to leave very early tomorrow morning, we decided that Neena should sleep over at my house tonight. Everwood is SO far away, basically the other side of the country, which is why we don't visit that often.

"Just one last thing to pack!" Neena slides a black leather journal into her backpack – her Jinncyclopedia.

Neena's uncle passed down the old book to her. It contains the records of countless Dreamweavers over the last one hundred years. It's called a Jinncyclopedia as it has details of all the different types of jinn (that we know of) within its yellowed pages.

Neena made me my own Jinncyclopedia that she translated into English. It's much slimmer than Neena's since she only put the most important information in, and it would take years to translate all the pages in hers! I'm looking forward to building mine up to be just as epic. Maybe I'll even pass it on to my own dreamweaving apprentice one day…

"Ready, Mum," Neena said. She runs up to Ameena and wraps her arms around her. "I'll miss you, though. Are you sure you'll be OK here?"

I know that Neena isn't just worried about her mum missing her. Since the Bhoot ramped up his efforts to get Neena to join his evil alliance of Soothsayers, we've been on high alert. We know that he's planning to merge the spirit world with the human world and that Neena is "the key" to that happening – whatever that means. Exactly *why* he wants to merge the worlds remains a mystery.

"I'm sure Grandma and I will be perfectly fine," Ameena says, stroking Neena's head with one hand. "And so will you and so will everyone in the town. It's only for one week, and didn't you say Tiff and Murray are away for the holidays too?"

I nod. Our best friends Tiff and Murray both left this evening to go and stay with their families for Christmas. Murray has gone to his uncle's house and Tiff is flying to South Korea to stay with her grandparents. If they're far away, hopefully the Bhoot won't be able to target them to get to Neena. Not that they know about any of this stuff anyway... I'll really miss them both but it's much easier to talk to Neena about dreamweaving without having to whisper or write secret notes to each other.

"So everyone is perfectly safe," Ameena says with a forced smile. "And you children need to have fun!"

Neena and I catch each other's eye, and I can see a glint of worry in her look. To be honest, I'm uneasy too. I've got better at managing my inner scaredy-cat but leaving Ameena and Neena's grandma – the only other Soothsayers I know – is a frightening thought.

"And since the Bhoot doesn't know who Tito is, I suppose we're safer away at his grandparents' house anyway," Neena reasons.

My stomach flips. I *may* have been *kind of* avoiding telling Neena that the Bhoot does in fact know who I am – he saw me and heard my name the last time we ran into him. OK, I've *totally* been avoiding it – she would be so worried! But it may be better if Ameena and Neena knew…

Then I think of being at the seaside with my family and my best friend, in the most fun place ever. Maybe I can wait until *after* this week to break the news. I don't want anything to ruin the best holiday ever.

"Neeeeeena, Tiiiiiito!" my mama sings up the stairs. Mama loves opera and likes to let people know – no matter where she is!

Ameena chuckles. "Your mama is waiting. Come."

I'm a little relieved that the moment to talk about the Bhoot has passed. Ameena ushers us down the stairs and I take one last look at Neena's room.

We'll be back in a week. Just one week. What could possibly go wrong?

CHAPTER TWO
WELCOME TO SNORESVILLE

After three long hours of motorways, multiple rounds of I spy and listening to Mama's rendition of "Nessun dorma" (and she *really* belted out the high notes) we are all fed up of travelling. But as Nan and Grandad live so far away, there's still one more hour to go.

My mum and mama have taken it in turns to drive but I can tell they're both tired too. They've been drinking lots of black coffee from a Thermos.

"Lello!" my baby brother Roberto says,

pointing at a yellow car out of the window.

He's only two so he's sitting in a car seat in between me and Neena. He also seems to be the only one still having fun. Everyone says he's like a mini-me; we have the same light brown curly hair, big brown eyes and button nose. I also have a sneaking suspicion that he may be a Dreamweaver too, but he's too young to tell yet.

"Yes, 'yellow'. And in Italiano?" Mama says.

I whisper in Roberto's ear, "Giallo."

Roberto just babbles – I don't think he's got the hang of Italian yet.

"I wish Rupert could have come with us," I say, looking out at the fields beside the motorway. "I bet he'd love the seaside."

Rupert is my labradoodle and unofficial second brother. Even though I begged and pleaded to bring him with us, Mum's work friend is looking after him while we are on holiday.

"I know, love." Mum sighs. "The drive is just too far for him – it's bad enough for us! It's why we haven't been for so long. But it's worth it when we get there."

Mama chuckles. "It certainly is. You two won't want to leave!"

Neena and I smile at each other. One week of fun, coming right up!

We drive on
until the fields
outside start
to become
dotted with
houses
and then
finally –
"The
sea!"
Neena
gasps.

A dark blue expanse of water stretches to the horizon visible from Neena's window. I suddenly realize something. "Neena, is this your first time seeing the sea since coming to the UK?"

Neena nods. "I wonder how cold it is? I've never been in the ocean."

Mum is looking at Neena in the rear-view mirror and smiling. Then I notice her wink at Mama. She's planning something!

"I tell you what, since we aren't supposed to be at Nan and Grandad's until the evening, how about we stop at the fairground first? It's right on the beachfront so you could also have a paddle, if you're brave enough. It will be freezing!"

Neena and I cheer, which makes Roberto clap his hands together too. That's a definite *yes*. A fizzing excitement fills my stomach and then spreads all the way through my body. My parents are the *best*.

We stop in a small car park in the town centre and wrap up warm in our coats. It's very cold and windy, but that doesn't stop me and Neena from running all the way down the promenade towards the fairground rides in the distance. I hear Roberto whinging behind us as he's buckled firmly in his pushchair.

"Tito?" Neena pants, as we come to a stop outside the entrance. "Are the people in Everwood always so … zombie-like?"

I raise my eyebrows. *What is she talking about?* But then I look around.

There are only a few groups of people out walking on the promenade but all of them are trudging slowly along, with long, drooping faces and sunken eyes. They are barely speaking to each other except for the odd grunt.

"Uhhh, I don't really remember – I was really young when we last visited. Maybe?"

"Are you both ready for the funfair?" Mama beams, finally catching up. "The entrance gates are just over— Oh!"

We've turned on to the ramp that connects the promenade to the pier where the fairground is, but the gates are closed. Big silver chains are wound through the bars and a huge padlock hangs off the end.

"Closed?" I cry out. "But it's supposed to be open three hundred and sixty-five days a year!"

We all look at a sign pinned to the gates. Mum reads it out loud for us:

"Mr Archibald, owner of the Fantasmic Funtime Fairground, has closed the amusements for the foreseeable future to pursue his new passion of reading the newspaper and eating dry toast. Goodbye."

My heart sinks and I look at Neena in despair. Her brow is crumpled but then she forces a smile. "It's OK, I'm sure there's still loads of other fun things for us to do, right?"

"Sì, there is much to do," Mama says, clipping a grumbling Roberto back into his pushchair. "Why don't we try the arcade instead? I've been saving up my tenpence coins for you."

I take a deep breath and nod. Right. The fairground might be closed but there's still the arcade. We can have loads of fun there.

We walk back the way we came along the promenade, to where there's a small parade of gift shops, a fish-and-chip shop and the arcade. As we walk I pay more attention to the people that we pass. They do seem lifeless, and their skin is almost grey. Is Everwood not as fun as it is in my memory?

We reach the arcade and I breathe a sigh of relief. The shutters are up and it's open!

"Let's do the racing car game first!" I call to Neena, before running ahead.

"Wait for me!" she shouts back, chasing after me.

I run inside, expecting to be met with
the noise and multicoloured flashing lights
of the arcade games, and stop dead. Something's
different. It's really dim inside, only a few bare
lightbulbs hang from the ceiling. I spin around
on the spot and notice, with horror, that most of
the games are powered down and boarded up!

"What's going on?" I groan.

"I think that game's still running," Neena
says, pointing to an area at the end of the arcade.

I squint to read the sign. *Golf simulator*.

"Noooooo, that's so boring!" I cry out,
covering my face with my hands.

Mum and Mama come in behind us and
look at the surroundings.

"Well, this has changed," Mum says quietly.
"What's happened to all the games?"

Mama walks over to the left side of the
hall and studies a wall. "You won't believe
this – they have a sign saying 'watch paint dry!'
as if it's one of the games."

"No way." Neena gawps. "That isn't normal, is it?"

I shake my head firmly. "None of this is normal."

"At least there's solitaire?" Mum shrugs, pointing at an impossibly chunky old computer in the corner with some pixelated cards on the screen.

"Mum, that looks like it was made in two thousand and five or something." I groan.

"I'm so sorry, Neena, it used to be much more fun, I promise."

Mum and Mama look concerned.

"I don't know what's happened to the place," Mum agrees with me. "We're sorry, loves. Maybe we should just get to Nan and Grandad's?"

But Mama claps her hands together. "I have an idea! Everyone back to the car – there's one more place we haven't tried."

We march back outside and pile into the car, feeling very defeated. But as Mama drives through the town centre and stops outside a large blue building with white foamy waves painted on to the side, I feel a flutter of hope in my chest.

"The Sea Life centre!" I smile.

"The place where we can touch a starfish, right?" Neena asks. "Yay!"

There's a small queue to enter the Sea Life centre and I notice Mum and Mama nudging each other and pointing at the other visitors in the line. A pale older man in beige clothes holds his wife's hand limply. Neither one of them are smiling. A teenage girl is observing her wristwatch tick with a blank expression. The family in front of us are dressed in matching brown overalls, occasionally sighing at each other. Neena's right, the people here are acting strangely...

We buy our tickets and follow the queue around into the main hall. This is where the starfish tank is – I remember because the ceiling above is decked out in star-shaped lights, although none of them are twinkling today. Neena and I wait our turn until we're called to the front, then we reach out our hands, dunk them in the tank and see –

"Ew, what's that?" Neena asks, pulling out her hand quickly.

Inside the large, circular pool, filled with moss and coral, is *one single sea snail*.

"Excuse me, where are the rest of the exhibits?" Mum says, a little sharply, to a teenage boy in staff uniform sitting next to the tank.

"This is our exhibit," the boy replies in a monotone voice.

"One snail? ONE SNAIL?" Mama exclaims. "I could see this in my garden at home! Come, we're getting our money back."

"Snail! Snail!" Roberto cheers and Mum pats him on the head.

"Not now, darling," she whispers.

Mama marches us angrily back to the entrance and as we go, I notice all the other tanks in the room are empty. We get our money back (no one dares argue with Mama when she starts ranting in Italian) and file back into the car.

For a moment we sit in silence before tears brim in my eyes. "I'm sorry, Neena," I sniffle. "I really wanted this to be a fun holiday for you."

Neena reaches over Roberto to squeeze my hand. "Don't worry, Tito, we'll still have fun. The holiday has only just started."

One of Neena's special talents – besides dreamweaving! – is finding the bright side in every situation. Just seeing her smile helps me feel a bit better about the fairground failure and the arcade flop.

We pull out of the car park and drive towards Nan and Grandad's house. I have a sinking feeling in my stomach from the disappointment of the day, but I try to rouse myself. "I can't wait to see Nan and Grandad.

I bet they have something really fun planned."

"Knowing my dad, I bet he'll have a prank ready for when you walk in," Mum laughs. "Remember the 'fun button', Tito?"

I start giggling. "Oh yeah! Grandad has a mole on his forehead that he calls his fun button. If you press it, he pretends he's a robot that's malfunctioning."

Neena's eyes go wide and she starts cracking up.

"And Tito's nan has an amazing collection of board games," Mama adds, looking at Neena in the rear-view mirror. "You can choose to play whatever you want."

Neena and I smile at each other. Maybe this holiday can be saved after all.

Maybe there is some fun left in Everwood.

CHAPTER THREE
JUST ANOTHER PRANK?

Nan and Grandad's house isn't far from
the town centre so it's just a short drive
to the cosy cul-de-sac where they live.
There are ten bungalows in the close,
each with a pretty little garden out front.
I've always liked how the bungalows match
and the gardens fit together nicely in neat
green squares.

At Christmas they all put lights and
decorations outside their houses and it looks
like Santa's grotto – although I notice this
year the gardens are bare and the bungalows

undecorated. That's strange.

We pull up into the drive next to
Grandad's old car and I rush to get my
seat belt off.

"I can't wait to see Nan and Grandad!"
I cheer, opening the car door ready to sprint
to the house.

"Take Neena with you," Mama reminds
me.

Oops! Of course, Neena has never been
here before. I wait for Neena to grab her bag
and then we both hurry to the front door.
I reach up and press the button, which plays
a funny jingle.

Neena laughs. "I've never heard a musical
doorbell before."

There's movement inside the house and
I hear Nan's voice as she turns the key.
"Must get that annoying bell changed..."
we hear her mumble, then the door opens.
"Hello."

"Nan!" I shout, throwing my arms around her. She pats me on the back.

"Hello, Tito," she says in a flat voice. "Hello, Neena. Welcome to our house."

Then she turns and gestures for us to enter.

Neena looks at me with a concerned expression.

It takes me a second but then I get it. "Ohhhh this must be part of their prank!" I laugh. "Come on, let's find Grandad."

We walk past Nan, further into the bungalow, to the large living room. Grandad is sitting in his armchair with a small table in front of him. He's concentrating on a magazine.

"Grandad, we're here," I announce.

I hear Mum, Mama and Roberto coming in the front door and greeting Nan.

Grandad looks up from his magazine, his eyes drooping. "Oh, hello." Then his gaze lowers and he starts writing.

"I'm not sure what this prank is," I whisper to Neena. "But it's not as fun as their usual ones."

Neena's brow is furrowed and her mouth pressed into a thin line. This must be quite awkward for her.

"Hiya, Dad," Mum says, bustling into the room with armfuls of luggage. "How are you?"

Grandad looks up and grunts.

"Charming!" Mum laughs. She looks at the piece of paper Grandad is focusing on. "Sudoku? But you've always teased me for doing those! I believe your words were 'it's for people who don't know how to have fun'."

"We've got into it recently," Nan says, sitting down on a floral sofa.

"Well… I'm glad. I suppose interests change as you get older," Mum says, looking sideways at Mama.

Neena is still standing awkwardly in the middle of the room, holding on to her backpack tightly.

"Grandad, this is my friend Neena," I say, trying to get the fun started. "Maybe we could all play a game."

Grandad frowns. "Oh, I can't do that. I'll miss the clock turning to half past."

Grandad points at the big clock on the wall that's ticking loudly. In fact, I realize that's the *only* sound I can hear. Usually they have a record playing or the radio on Groovin' 60s.

"Uh, Tito, why don't you take Neena to set up your camp-beds?" Mum says quickly.

Feeling deflated, I lead Neena to the end of the corridor where Grandad's "office" is. It's a small room with a desk, computer and Grandad's model railway set, but he's packed away the railway to make room for me and Neena.

"Tito, do your grandparents not like me?" Neena asks in a small voice.

"No, no, it's not that at all!" I reply. "They were so excited you were coming when I spoke to them on the phone last week. They've changed. They used to be so much fun, I promise."

"I believe you. Do you think something strange is going on? Something … magical?"

My stomach flips. In the past year, we've seen our friends swap personalities and our teachers become cranky and tired from jinn infiltrating their dreams. Could something similar be happening here?

"I hope not." I shudder. "Maybe we can snap them out of it? Get Grandad and Nan to have fun again?"

"Good idea," Neena agrees. "Then we can decide whether it's something serious or just them getting older, like your mum says."

We unpack our bags, lay out duvets on the beds and then decide on who gets to sleep by the window by doing rock, paper scissors.

Soon it's dinner time and Mama has made spaghetti bolognese. She calls it her "easy meal" for when she's tired, but Mama is such a great chef that everything she makes tastes like it must have taken hours to prepare.

We all eat together, mostly in silence, apart from Roberto who babbles in between bites of spaghetti that he eats with his chubby hands. Nan and Grandad barely say anything apart from complaining that the food has "too much flavour". Mama does her best not to be offended but I notice her cheeks flush as she spoons plain spaghetti on to plates for them. They usually *love* Mama's cooking.

After dinner Mum and Mama put Roberto to bed in his travel cot and Nan decides to go to bed too (at 8 p.m.!). With no change in his behaviour yet, Neena and I decide it's time to try to get Grandad back to his old fun self.

"Grandad, we found this game in Nan's board game cupboard," I ask tentatively. "It's called Mouse Chase. Do you want to play?"

"No, thank you, I'd rather listen to the

clock tick," Grandad replies, sitting in his armchair with his hands folded in his lap. His eyes are half closed and I can tell he *really is* listening to the seconds go by. How is that fun?!

Neena glances at me before trying herself. "Why don't we just set up in here and you can join in if you feel like it?"

We unbox the game on the table in front of Grandad and pull up two chairs. As we're getting out the pieces, I see Grandad's eyes light up.

"I'd like to be the yellow mouse!" he says suddenly.

"Great!" Neena cheers.

"I'll be red." I smile.

We start playing and Grandad joins in, slowly at first but then getting more and more into it. At one point he rolls two sixes and jumps up out of his chair and whoops, "Oh yeah!" He does a little dance.

Maybe everything is going to be OK after all. I roll the dice and end up in the mouse jail.

"Ha ha," Grandad says, sticking out his tongue. He nudges Neena and she copies him, the two of them laughing.

"This is great." I laugh along. "I'm having so much fun!"

Suddenly Grandad's smile drops and his laughs slow to a halt. "Yes… Yeah, I—"

41

His eyelids droop and his shoulders hunch over. "I think the game is finished now."

Neena and I look at each other with wide eyes. What happened? I motion Neena to join me in the kitchen and we huddle in a corner so we won't be overheard.

"That was weird," I whisper. "Something definitely isn't right. He was having fun, laughing loads and then it was like—"

"All the fun got zapped out of him," Neena says, finishing my sentence.

I've seen enough weird things happen since becoming a Dreamweaver to know there's something fishy going on under the surface, in the dream realm.

"I think," I say with a big sigh, "we need to dreamweave into my grandad's dream tonight."

Neena nods, her eyes blazing. "I agree. I mean, I feel awkward because it's your grandad, but we shouldn't take any chances."

I peer back into the living room where Grandad is sitting, just staring at a blank wall, the discarded Mouse Chase game lying sadly in front of him. That's not my fun grandad – something's happened to him.

And I'm going to get to the bottom of it.

CHAPTER FOUR
GRANDAD'S DREAM

Mama tucks me into the foldout camp-
bed and gives me a kiss on the cheek.
"Buonanotte, sogni d'oro."

Mama turns to Neena sleeping on the
camp-bed next to the window. "And sweet
dreams to you, darling. Don't stay up too
late talking."

As Mama moves over to the door she
yawns and I notice bags under her eyes. It
has been a long day; she must be tired from
all the driving. She and Mum are sleeping in
the spare room with Roberto in his travel cot

next to them. But knowing my little brother, he'll find a way to wriggle into their bed.

Neena rolls over to face me when the door is closed. "Did you get an item from your grandad?" she whispers.

To dreamweave into someone *else's* dream, you have to be holding a belonging of theirs as you fall asleep. I reach down under my bed and grab the smooth round object I'd swiped from the living room.

"I've got his lucky cricket ball," I say, holding it up in the dark room. I rub my thumb over the stitching that runs round the middle of the leather ball. "Grandad won a match with this when he was younger."

"That's perfect," says Neena. "My cousins and uncles used to play cricket at home in the village. I never understood much, though…"

Neena's voice sounds sleepy and I can tell she'll drift off soon. We've both already drawn our dream symbols on our hands before bed so we can enter each other's dreams. Our emoji symbols are like magical keys to the dream realm.

"Meet you in my dream, yeah?" I say quickly, before Neena falls asleep.

"Mmhmm," Neena mumbles.

I turn over on to my side and try to get comfy but the bed is hard and springy from being folded up in a cupboard. I can hear Neena's soft snores coming from behind me and it's strangely comforting. It helps me feel calm and kind of heavy until slowly … I start … to…

"Tito!"

My eyes blink open and I'm standing in

Titotown on my magical clifftop. The grass is cold and soft under my bare feet and the sky is filled with swirling neon colours. It's night-time and I'm wearing my pyjamas, so I weave myself into my dreamweaving outfit – purple baggy trousers and a long-sleeved top.

I turn towards the pine-tree forest where Neena is standing, hands on her hips. "Where have you been?" she shouts out. "I've been waiting ages!"

"It's only been like five minutes in normal time," I say, walking over to her. "Your snoring kept me awake!"

Neena whacks me on the arm but I can see she's smirking. "Are you ready for this?" she says. "Going into your grandad's dream must feel weird, but we are only doing it because of—"

"Special circumstances." I nod, finishing her sentence. "I'm sure, I'm ready."

Going into someone else's dream is an

invasion of privacy and should only be done if it's a last option – that was one of the first rules of dreamweaving that Neena taught me. But after seeing how much Everwood has changed and how my grandparents have turned into weird boring versions of themselves, I need to find out what's going on.

I put my hand in the deep pocket of my baggy trousers and hold the cricket ball firmly. Then I picture my grandad in my mind and imagine his gruff laugh as he pretends to produce a coin out of thin air from behind my ear, or pokes me in the tickly spot under my ribs. I hold out both hands, palms up, as golden sparks appear in the air in front of me. They grow and spread into a large black portal surrounded by the fizzling sparks.

A portal that leads into Grandad's dream.

It's big enough for Neena and me to step through so we hold hands and walk in.

At once, we're sucked into the dark and for a moment we float motionless in thin air, before dropping back down on to solid ground.

Light floods my eyes and it takes a while for them to adjust.

Surrounding us are green fields bathed in sunlight and one large field of yellow wheat. We're standing outside a small stone building with a wooden roof. Next to it an ancient tractor lies haphazardly on its side.

"Is it a farm?" Neena asks, peering around.

I shrug. "Looks like it. Come on, let's try to find Grandad."

We walk up to the front door and creak it open, not sure what we're going to find. Everything looks normal so far – even quite peaceful. But something about just *how normal* everything seems makes the hairs on my neck prick up.

We walk inside and immediately notice a boy around our age sitting at a long wooden table. He's fiddling around with a toy aeroplane, and tiny pots of paint and brushes are scattered in front of him. As soon as he hears the door creak he looks up and sees us.

Busted.

Neena and I freeze. We aren't sure who the boy is – what if he's some kind of jinn in disguise who has hijacked my grandad's dream?

"Hello, who are you?" the boy says.

"Um…" Neena takes the lead. "I'm Neena and this is Tito."

The boy's confusion breaks and he grins widely. "Oh *yes*, of course, I know you. Would you like to play?"

Neena and I walk over to the table and sit down, a little unsure what to do. We can't exactly leave. It would seem odd, plus we really should try to investigate to find out what's going on.

We both pick up a paintbrush and the boy hands us a wooden wing each.

"I love planes," the boy says. "Have you ever been on a plane?"

"I have," Neena says, her eyes narrowed. She's suspicious of the boy too.

But that's when I notice it. A mole right in the middle of the boy's forehead. A memory flashes in my mind and suddenly it starts to make sense where we are.

"I remember my grandad saying he grew up on a farm," I whisper to Neena. "He must be dreaming about his childhood! And look at that mole, it's the fun button. Which means…"

Neena looks from me, to the boy, then back to me again. "Oh my gosh – he's your… That's your…"

"Grandad!" I breathe, my eyes wide.

"Tito!" The boy reaches out across the table. "Come on, let's play."

Suddenly Grandad, well *child* Grandad, grabs one of the finished planes and jumps up on to the table! He flies the plane through the air, making *whooshing* noises and pretending to crash-land on to Neena's head.

Neena and I laugh along, in complete shock and joy at being able to play with Grandad when he's the same age as us.

"This is amazing!" Neena says in awe.

"Mum always says Nan and Grandad are kids at heart," I say, looking up at Grandad nosediving his plane only to scoop it back into the air at the last moment.

"Well, it looks like there isn't a problem with his inner world," Neena says quietly to me. "He's still having fun in here."

But no sooner have the words left her mouth than a strange grey mist materializes on the other side of the table and swarms on the spot, becoming darker and more solid, until a thin, pale figure appears. It's about six feet tall, bald, with small eyes and a tiny nose. It's dressed in a long black cape that drapes its body from neck to feet. It's so weird looking that my mouth falls open in confusion.

"*What. Is. That?*" I whisper.

Before Neena can answer, the creature puckers its lips and puffs out its cheeks. It looks like an alien-pufferfish hybrid! It starts to make a loud, wet sucking noise as if it was slurping a slushie. If I wasn't so shocked, I think I would have burst out laughing.

Rainbow-coloured waves of energy start draining from child Grandad, whose back is turned to the creature. His laughter subsides, just as it did when we played Mouse Chase. Then his arms drop to his sides, the plane clattering to the table. He crumples down and slides on to his chair, eyes drooping and smile wiped clean from his face. His skin has turned a horrible grey colour that sends a shiver down my back.

"Hey!" I shout angrily. "Stop that!"

I'm surprised when the creature does abruptly stop. It rubs its stomach and licks its lips, then vanishes *poof* in a puff of grey smoke. I turn to face Neena who is standing frozen to the spot, her fists curled in anger.

"Tito, we have to go," she says steadily, backing away from the table.

It's like the colour has started to seep out of the world. The grey and white eats up the colours of the kitchen, spreading towards us rapidly.

"Snap out of it, Grandad!" I yell, but he doesn't seem able to hear me.

Neena grabs me and pulls me towards the door. We run outside and head over to the wheat field where the bursting yellow colours are still intact and the sun shining.

"What was that *thing*, Neena? What did it do to my grandad?" I pant, looking back over at the house, which is losing its colour before my eyes.

Neena has started pacing back and forth, shaking her head. When she hears me speak, though, she stops and holds her hand out. The Jinncyclopedia materializes within it.

"I know what it is," she says gravely. "Though I've never seen one in real life."

She flicks through the pages until she finds the right entry then starts translating aloud. I can't believe what I'm hearing.

"It's a vampire?" I immediately interrupt. "Like the scary Dracula kind?"

"No. Those kinds of vampires are *sooo* fake." Neena rolls her eyes. "Let me read the rest."

Vampire

Appearance: pale, thin, tall, bald, often dressed in black, human-like with almost alien features.

Behaviour: solitary hunters that feed on funergy, attracted to laughter, rarely seen, hard to engage in conversation, possibly endangered as the world becomes more boring.

Strengths: can move between the spirit world and dream world effortlessly, can shift between a fine mist and solid.

Weaknesses: bright sunlight, boredom.

Notable Sightings:
1940 - Kameni, Santorini, sulphur hot springs
1952 - New Orleans, swing bar
1983 - Eastern Transylvania, castle ruins
1994 - Kuldhara ghost village, India

A shiver runs all the way from my back up to my scalp. "They feed on funergy?" I ask Neena. "Is that like … *blood?*"

Neena shakes her head. "Real vampires don't suck blood, they suck *fun.*"

My hands fly to my face as it all comes together. I sit down heavily on the floor, feeling completely shocked. "So the entire town of Everwood and everyone in it, including my grandparents, are having the fun sucked out of them?"

"It looks like it. And the effects are strong even in the waking world." Neena sits down next to me. "This must be one hungry vampire."

CHAPTER FIVE
FAMILY SURPRISES

I wake up the next morning with my legs hanging off the camp-bed and my head squashed against Grandad's desk.

"Ouch." I groan, rubbing my neck.

"Yeah, that didn't look comfortable!" Neena is sitting on the edge of her camp-bed, already dressed.

"How long have you been awake?" I ask, yawning. I try to remember everything that happened last night. Wheat fields, aeroplanes and vampires rush through my mind. I shiver, even wrapped in my duvet.

"I couldn't sleep much after we saw the vampire," Neena says, biting her fingernails. "It's so strange. Why would it be causing trouble *here* in Everwood at the same time as we come to visit? It seems too much of a coincidence."

"You don't think… Could it be your uncle again?" I swallow hard, my throat dry from sleep and the fear that creeps up my spine whenever I think of the Darkweaver.

Neena shakes her head. "But why would my uncle target Everwood? He doesn't know who you are and he can't be accessing my dreams, he doesn't know my symbol."

A heavy feeling sinks like a stone in the pit of my stomach. I wanted to wait until after the holiday, but with everything that's happening now, I *have* to come clean.

Taking a big breath, I sit up in bed and face Neena.

"Actually, there's something I need to tell you," I say quietly. "The last time we faced the Bhoot, when he appeared inside the portal, he saw my face and he heard you say my name."

Neena's face goes pale. "S-so … the Bhoot *does* know who you are?"

I nod grimly. "I'm sorry, Neena, he could be using me to get to you. It's my fault the vampire is here."

The Bhoot has been tracking Neena ever

since she moved to the UK and sending
various jinn to try to capture her and bring
her to the alliance. A mysterious vampire
jinn in Everwood fits the pattern. Neena's
gaze clouds over for a moment as she's lost in
thought, but she shakes herself and her green
eyes blaze once more.

"It's not your fault, Tito, it's the Bhoot.
He has caused all this. I'm just sorry your
family have suffered because of his evil plan.
I should have been more careful to protect
you."

"We'll protect each other," I say firmly.
"But let's start with my grandparents."

"Yes, of course." Neena nods, but I still
see a hint of fear in her eyes.

I quickly change into a jumper and
jeans while Neena brushes her teeth.
My tummy rumbles as I think of breakfast.
Dreamweaving can really work up an
appetite. Usually when we come to visit,

Nan makes us a full English breakfast with eggs, sausages and beans that she arranges in a smiley face. Or maybe Mama will take over the cooking and make pancakes – she loves them almost as much as me!

We walk through the silent house to the kitchen where just the occasional clack of cutlery and Roberto's whinging can be heard. No radio on, no sizzle of sausages in the pan… Not a great sign.

"Good morning," Neena says brightly.

Mum, Mama and Roberto are all sitting at the round kitchen table. Nan is at the counter stirring the palest cup of tea I've ever seen – I'm worried it might just be milk and hot water – and Grandad is scraping salt on to an untoasted bagel.

Please tell me that isn't breakfast.

I look closer at my parents and my heart drops at seeing how pale and tired they look. Neither of them even glance up.

"Berto," I say, going over to my little brother's highchair and tapping him on the nose with my finger. "Good morning."

Berto doesn't react, he just looks up at me and says a quiet, "Hewo."

Neena reaches for my hand and squeezes it – I'm trying not to cry. My whole family have had the fun and laughter leeched out of them!

Neena and I sit at the table and Grandad puts two pieces of limp bagel in front of us, the most boring bland breakfast I've ever set eyes on.

"Any jam?" I ask.

"Jam!?" Nan gags at the suggestion.

I get up and manage to find some at the back of the fridge, while Neena tries to lift the mood.

"So have you listened to any opera today?" Neena asks Mama. "We could sing that duet you like about the flowers?"

Mama just sighs and sips her sad pale tea.

I try to help Neena and turn my attention on Mum with the biggest smile I can muster. "Oh, Mum, it's ten thirty – *DIY-YOUR-LIFE* will be on TV! Shall we watch it?"

Mum lifts her head slowly as if it's extremely heavy. "No, thanks, Tito. I'll just do sudoku with Nan and Grandad."

I swallow hard. This is worse than I thought – Mama not wanting to sing opera and Mum not interested in her favourite show? Neena's right, this vampire is really strong!

Neena gets up and beckons me into the living room, deep frown lines etched into her forehead. "It's affecting everybody," she whispers. "Even Roberto, though he doesn't seem as bad as the rest."

I look at my baby brother, who's pushing a little toy car around the table of his highchair. He seems less hyper than usual but he's still playing, so that's a good sign.

I sit down on the sofa heavily. "Maybe adults feel it worse because they already have less fun?"

"Maybe," Neena agrees, flopping down next to me.

Just then, Grandad appears in the doorway between the kitchen and the living room, scratching at his stubbly beard.

"Tito, Neena..." Grandad is looking at us, his eyes moving quickly from side to side. "Were you...? What game did we play last night?"

"We played Mouse Chase, remember?"
I reply.

"No, there was something else. Didn't
we play with an aeroplane?" Grandad shakes
his head and lowers himself into the leather
armchair.

Neena's eyes sparkle as she rushes forward
to sit on the floor in front of Grandad. "Yes,
we did. In your dream. Do you remember
that?" she asks breathlessly.

Suddenly Grandad's eyes widen and they
seem even bluer. He looks down at Neena
and then over to me. A smile spreads across
his face. "Tito," he says in a quiet voice.
"You're a Dreamweaver, aren't you?"

I feel like someone has dumped a bucket of
ice water over my head. "How do you know
about Dreamweavers?" I whisper, my heart
beating wildly.

Grandad looks over his shoulder towards
the kitchen where Mum, Mama and Nan

are still sitting in silence, then slaps his hands on his lap. "Right," he announces loudly. "Neena, Tito and I are going on a walk! And we'll need sandwiches."

He springs to his feet and Neena and I don't hesitate to follow him. I'm so relieved to see my grandad acting more like himself again that I don't push him for any more answers. Not now, at least.

While Grandad quickly whips up a few peanut butter sandwiches, Neena squeezes my shoulders with both hands and beams at me.

"Do you know what's going on?" I ask quietly.

She screws her nose up and smiles. "I have a *theory*. But we should let your grandad explain. This is good, Tito!"

She puts the sandwiches in her backpack then goes to get her trainers and coat.

I'm left standing in the living room,

confused. What is happening?

Grandad leads me and Neena out of their little close, back to the high street. "Bit dead around here today, isn't it," Grandad says, looking at the closed shops and zombie-like people who mill around aimlessly.

We head all the way up the high street towards the Everwood woods (I don't think they really thought that name through!). It's a grey and cloudy day, like it might start raining at any moment, and there's a cool wind. The whole time we're walking I just want to blurt out — "*How do you know about Dreamweavers!?*" — but I keep my cool and wait for Grandad to explain in his own time.

"In the mood for a hike?" He winks, pointing at the hill that slopes up from the wood's edge.

"Definitely." Neena smiles and I nod.

As we head into the woods and up the hill, the breeze disappears and the air grows still, sheltered by the dense trees and grass.

Grandad clears his throat. "I should explain," he begins.

"Yes, please!" I blurt out, making Grandad laugh.

"So. The reason I know that you're a

Dreamweaver, Tito, and you too I'm assuming, dear Neena, is because I am a Spiritlink."

"I knew it!" Neena yells and a flock of birds scatter from a nearby tree. "Oops, sorry."

I stop in my tracks and look at them both, astonished. "What on earth is a Spiritlink?"

Neena rummages in her backpack and pulls out her Jinncyclopedia triumphantly. "Aha!" She flicks to a page near the end. "Remember I told you there are lots of different types of Soothsayers? Well, Spiritlinks are one of them. I thought your Grandad might be a Soothsayer. I didn't know which kind for sure, but because he knew about Dreamweavers and the trait usually runs in families it made sense…"

Neena holds up the Jinncyclopedia and starts to translate it aloud:

Soothsayers are individuals who possess a magical ability. There are many types of Soothsayer and their powers vary greatly depending on personality, skill, likes and dislikes and many other factors. In general, we know of five main groups:

Dreamweavers: can access the dream realm as if they are awake, control their dreams and enter the dreams of others.

Healers: can heal physical and spiritual wounds or illness using natural materials and incantations.

Starreaders: can find out information about the past, present or future from reading the stars.

Spiritlinks: can communicate with spirits in the spirit world and sense when a spirit is nearby. Spiritlinks are versed in the languages of all jinn they encounter, talented individuals can also see the jinn they communicate with.

Spellcasters: the rarest form of Soothsayer, can cast spells on humans and jinn using incantations.

I gaze at Grandad as if I'm seeing him for the first time. My grandad, with his grey hair, silly sense of humour and red anorak – a Spiritlink!

I run up and throw my arms around him, squeezing him tight.

"Oof." Grandad pats my head and hugs me back. "Sorry I didn't tell you, Tito, but you know how it is being a Soothsayer, we have to be careful. Nan isn't one and neither is your mum so I could never say anything, but it must have skipped a generation and gone to you!"

"This is amazing!" Neena cheers and she joins in the hug, almost knocking us over. "But you should know. There's a vampire on the loose in Everwood. He's been sucking the fun out of the whole town – including you!"

Grandad's face goes pale and he rubs his chin with concern. "Well, that would explain why I've been feeling so odd. Come to think of it…" He lifts his face to the sky and starts looking around, turning in circles, almost as if he's sniffing the air. It reminds me of Rupert when he smells Mama cooking bacon. "I can sense lots of spirits nearby. More than I ever have here before. Come on, let's climb to the top of the hill. The last time you were there, Tito, I had to carry you. You were so little!"

We trudge upwards on the winding dirt path that's been etched into the hill from years of people walking this route. The wet weather of the past few days has made it muddy and squelchy underfoot, so we have to be extra careful not to slip.

"Hmm, yes, this must be a busy location in the spirit world today," Grandad says to us as he leads the way. "I sense lots of activity."

I remember how Neena explained the human world and the spirit world to me. It's kind of like the spirit world is an invisible map that exists on top of our world, but in another dimension. They're separated by an in-between realm so that humans and spirits don't cross into each other's worlds. The in-between realm is where dreams take place, and that's why we meet jinn there.

Even knowing that, the fact that Grandad can sense the spirit world on this damp, empty hill feels quite surreal.

I can tell we're nearing the top now as the pine trees are thinning out and the ground's more level. There's a fine drizzle in the air and it makes the pine smell fresh and earthy around us.

As we walk out on to the clifftop, a strange sensation comes over me. My skin prickles and my eyes widen.

The trees behind us, the grassy clifftop with the sky stretching above me and the sound of the waves crashing below. It's all very familiar...

I twist and turn to take in my surroundings. "This is... It can't be..."

But Neena sees it too and she takes me by the shoulders with both hands. "Tito, this is Titotown!"

"It's exactly the same as my dreambase," I breathe. "Only ... it's an actual place!" And that's not even the weirdest part.

CHAPTER SIX
TITOTOWN SQUARED

The clifftop is in magical pandemonium!

In the clearing before us, multiple dream portals are open. Actual dream portals in the waking world! They are small, no bigger than a football, and misshapen like they've been squashed.

"Are those…?" Neena doesn't finish her sentence.

Zipping in and out of the tiny portals are paris – fairies from the spirit world!

"Real–life jinn in the human world? Yep." I gulp.

But that's not all.

Over to our left, a fallen tree lies in
the damp grass. It'd be normal enough if it
weren't for the *human-sized hot dog singing
opera* on top of it! Before I can even react,
I hear insistent tweeting from the trees
above. I look up and see lots of small brown
sparrows in the branches, each with a perfect
twizzly moustache that curls up and down
with each note it chirps.

"Well, this is *very* odd," Grandad says,

squinting up at the sky. "And correct me if I'm wrong, but are those pizzas?"

Flying out of the portals like Frisbees are circular discs, spraying cheese and tomato sauce as they go. I inspect one that lands on the ground near my feet and notice it has a cardboard base.

I wish I could say that this was surprising, but I've seen all these things before. In fact, I've seen that racetrack at the edge of the clearing *very recently*.

"Neena, these are all things we've dreamweaved in Titotown before," I say, poking at the pizza. "The singing hot dog, the moustached birds, the cardboard pizzas and even the Titotown racetrack. They're all here! How is that possible? I have a bad feeling about this."

Neena turns her back to the chaos and shuts her eyes, as if blocking it out will help her think harder. "I said before that no one knows where dreambases come from, they're just *there* when a Dreamweaver firsts dreamweaves…" Neena opens her eyes. "But what if all dreambases are directly linked to places in the human world? I mean, mine is Chitral valley. I used to think it was just coincidence but now I'm not so sure."

I dodge a flying pizza and try to take in what Neena is saying. Could all dreambases in the dream realm also be places in the real world? What would that mean?

"Neena, can I get one of those sandwiches please? I have an idea," Grandad says, taking a seat on a nearby tree stump.

Neena rummages in her backpack to pull out one of the tightly wrapped sandwiches we packed for the hike.

"Right," Grandad begins. "Imagine the human world is the bottom slice of bread and the spirit world is the top slice of bread. The peanut butter in the middle is the dream realm, which is supposed to separate the two."

A few fairies flit over my head and I shoo them away, trying to concentrate on the sandwich.

"Well, what if dreambases are places where the barrier between the human world and spirit world is thin? Like this."

Grandad presses one finger down in the centre of the bread and it leaves a deep indentation where the two slices of bread and peanut butter are all smooshed together.

"But what if it was a cheese sandwich?" I ask, scratching my head.

"I think what your grandad is saying," Neena chimes in, "is that if dreambases exist in all three places: the human world, the dream realm and the spirit world, then it makes the barrier between them thin. So it's easier for things, like jinn, to pass through."

I nod slowly, taking it in. "I understand. But even if the barrier *is* thinner here on the clifftop, there shouldn't be peanut butter – I mean *jinn* – flying around and portals opening!"

"Exactly!" Neena exclaims. "The worlds have existed since time began and I've never heard of a problem like this happening before. The Bhoot must have done something to speed up his plan of merging the spirit world and human world."

"What's that about a boot?" Grandad says, frowning.

We have a *lot* to tell Grandad. But before we can start, closer to the cliff edge a gaggle of fairies start squabbling. They buzz loudly like an angry swarm of bees and I can hear their high-pitched voices shouting at each other.

Neena is about to rush over but Grandad holds up a hand. "I'll deal with this. I have spoken to many fairies in my time. Maybe I can convince them to go back to the spirit world."

I feel a flush of pride as my grandad walks over to the group of rainbow-coloured glowing figures. When Neena and I encountered a group of paris in the past, we had to speak to them in riddles and rhyme to get them to talk to us. But Grandad starts speaking in a language I've never heard before. It's kind of like a mix of French, Russian and yodelling!

"What is that?" I gasp.

"It's fairy language." Neena smiles. "Spiritlinks can speak the language of the jinn they encounter, though their ability starts off rough and gets better over time. Kind of like me when I learned English…"

The swarm seems to calm down as Grandad speaks and I relax. Maybe if all three of us work together, we can get the clifftop back under control. Grandad even starts to laugh, sharing a joke with the fairies. Suddenly a larger portal at the very tip of the cliff edge starts to wobble and stretch wider.

"Tito, look!" Neena gulps.

Inside the portal, the distinct shape of the vampire appears – and it's facing Grandad!

It purses its lips, blows out its cheeks and then comes that noise…

Sluuurrrpppppp.

"We have to stop it!" I shout, running towards Grandad, who is still chortling away with the fairies.

Colourful energy lines begin draining out of Grandad who is looking paler and paler, drooping to his knees. The vampire reaches out its hands, wiggling its long, spindly fingers as if it's trying to push through the portal on to our side – into the human world.

"Cut it out, you giggle gobbler!" I yell.

"Tito, here!" Neena calls from behind me.

I turn around just in time for her to throw me a long, sturdy tree branch. I sprint past Grandad, who is hunched over on the floor surrounded by fairies, and over to the large portal. Then I muster all my strength and jab the tree branch into the portal with a sharp thrust, hitting the vampire right in the chest.

"OOF," it wheezes. "That hurt!"

Then it turns and runs, disappearing
further back inside the portal.

I bend down next to Grandad. The fairies
are perched all over him, stroking his face
and playing with his hair. Their big bug eyes
are wide with concern. Slowly, a pink colour
returns to his cheeks. They're helping him!

Neena stands next to me, eyeing the large portal and staring into the murky depths.

"We have to follow it, right?" I say, not really wanting to hear the answer.

"It's the only way to know what's going on for sure," Neena replies.

I've never entered a portal from the human world before. I have no idea what's on the other side, or who has even created it. The smaller, football-sized portals look almost like tears in the sky, but this larger one is a perfect circle – almost deliberate. It seems silly to jump inside it. But I know we *have* to stop this vampire.

I stand next to Neena, sighing, and begin counting. "Three … two … one!"

Neena and I leap through the portal, right off the cliff edge. For a moment I'm convinced we'll plummet into the sea below, before I feel the familiar sensation of being held in space.

Just before we're sucked through to wherever this portal leads, I look back.

There, to my shock, I see mine and Neena's bodies, curled up on the grass, sound asleep.

Somehow that tops the list of absolutely crazy things I've seen today.

CHAPTER SEVEN
VAMPIRE CHASE

We land heavily on wet grass and I know
immediately that we're in Titotown –
my dream-realm version of the real-life
Everwood clifftop.

It's daytime and everything seems kind of
warped. The edges of things – the pine trees,
rocks, bushes and birds – are blurred. I want
to stop and inspect what's happened to my
dreambase but we can't. There's a vampire to
catch.

"The vampire is up ahead," Neena says,
grabbing my hand. "It's created a portal!"

We chase after the pale figure that floats through the air in a grey mist only to disappear into another swirling, jagged portal. There's no time to pause, no time to even think! We jump through the portal after it.

Our feet hit cold, hard earth and I feel a chill on my face. We keep running. It's a dark, starlit night but I can just make out dry desert land all around us, a few tall palm trees nearby and three large, triangular structures in the distance.

"Wait, are those the Pyramids?" I gasp, panting as we run after the vampire.

As soon as I point them out, the golden colour of each pyramid and the dark blue of the night sky starts to bleed out into a dull grey. The vampire is draining the fun of whoever's dream this is as it goes!

"Hey, Count Snore-cula, stop it!" Neena yells.

The vampire is at the bottom of a large sand dune now and about to leap into another portal it's created – we're going to lose it!

"Tito, look," Neena exclaims, pointing at a pile of discarded wood at the top of the dune.

As if we've read each other's minds, we leap on to the largest piece and push off, hurtling down the hill of sand at top speed.

Our makeshift toboggan is heading right to the portal.

"Here we go!" Neena cries out.

We zoom straight into the portal just as it's closing, then we're sucked in and spat out into another dream.

This one is a dense rainforest. The sound of chirruping bugs and hidden creepy-crawlies surrounds us and my skin itches.

"It's over there!" I urge, pointing out the vampire in the distance. It seems to have got caught up in some vines that have slowed it down. *Perfect.*

We tear our way through the thick foliage, pushing aside sprawling palm leaves and tripping over roots as we go. The vampire is *just* an arm's reach away from us now … but it manages to get loose and set off again at an alarmingly fast pace. *Ugh!*

"Whose dreams are these anyway?" I huff, whacking a heavy vine out of our way.

"No idea. Just keep running!" Neena replies breathlessly.

The rainforest up ahead thins out and, as

we get closer, I suddenly understand why.

"It's a canyon!" I screech, as the gaping chasm comes into view.

The vampire hurtles to a stop, pauses a moment and then turns into a grey mist! It floats across the other side of the canyon where it materializes again and continues sucking the air around it.

"I don't suppose you're able to turn into smoke?" I puff at Neena who's running alongside me.

She looks up at the towering trees on the edge of the canyon. "Nope, but I can do this – hold on!"

She grabs a particularly thick green vine dangling from a branch that overhangs the canyon. I wrap my hands around the vine and block out the voice in my head screaming "WHAT ON EARTH AM I DOING?" as we leap off the edge and swing across the sheer drop.

"Don't look down," I warble, more to myself than Neena.

We land on the other side and spy the vampire disappearing into another portal.

"We *definitely* have to talk about how awesome that was later," Neena pants. "But right now, keep chasing that vampire!"

We follow the creature into the portal then emerge in a field where a large, square-based stone pyramid stands. Huge steps lead up to a room at the top and dense trees line the field. The whole thing looks familiar and I swear I've seen this place on TV before but we don't stop – just jump after the vampire into yet *another* portal.

We pass through a doctor's surgery full of angry patients, run across the roof of a high school, paraglide off the top of the Eiffel Tower, hitch a ride on a tractor through the middle of Stonehenge and finally emerge on to a large viewing platform where the sound of crashing water fills the air.

The vampire has floated to the edge of the platform before it stops abruptly by the barriers and throws its hands up to shield its face. When we finally catch up with it, I see why.

We are at Niagara Falls on a brilliantly sunny morning! My mum and I watched a nature documentary about this place once – it's even more impressive in real life. Or at least, in dream life.

The huge waterfalls crash down below and the rising sun casts bright rays on to us from the horizon.

The vampire cowers and curls up in a ball on the floor. The sun is much too powerful for it to turn into smoke again.

"There's nowhere to run," Neena shouts over the sound of the water. "Tell us why you're draining Everwood! Why did the Bhoot send you?"

"*Whoooo?*" the vampire yells back, in a strange ghoulish voice that also sounds a bit like a trumpet.

"The Bhoot!" I shout back, not wanting to get any closer to the creature.

"Argh, this blasted sunlight," the vampire groans. "Help me!"

Neena sighs and starts weaving with her hands. Trees sprout from the ground and grow upwards in a circle around the three of us, blocking out the sunlight while also preventing the vampire from leaving.

"That's better." Neena brushes off her hands. "Now tell us the Bhoot's plan!"

The vampire finally stands up again, straightening out its black cape. It cocks its head to one side and blinks. "*Whooo* and *what* is the Bhoot? My plan is simple – I was bored and craved some delicious fun. Your dreambase was the easiest one on the grid to break into from the spirit world."

"What grid?" I mumble to Neena.

Neena shrugs and shakes her head.

"But as you surely know, the grid is most peculiar at the moment. There's more power surging through it than usual," the vampire continues. "Happily, it makes it much easier to break through to feed."

"Ew, gross." I shiver.

The vampire is inching closer to us, moving so slowly and softly it's basically gliding. "And that large portal on your clifftop looked especially promising… Like it was made just for me. I might be able to break through that one straight into the human world. Imagine all the scrumptious fun I could be feasting on, whenever my heart desires, not *just* when you are sleeping. Speaking of which…"

The vampire puckers its lips, puffs out its cheeks and takes a deep breath.

"It's going to drain us!" I say, grabbing

Neena and backing away.

But the trees Neena dreamweaved are so dense that we can't escape!

Think, Tito, think.

"What if I told you I know how you can get an endless supply of fun, without draining us?" I blurt out. I hold on to Neena tightly but my focus is solely on the vampire.

The vampire lets the air out of its cheeks and it sounds like a deflating balloon.

I have to stop myself from giggling. Why do I always want to laugh in the most serious situations?!

The vampire raises its eyesbrows. "Go on…"

"Well, the best thing about fun is it can never run out … if you make it yourself," I carry on, my voice shaking a little.

"Yeah, why waste time hunting people to feed on when you can make your own food?" Neena joins in, helping me, "Besides, we *need* fun in our world too. We can't live without it."

The vampire strokes its pointy chin with a long finger. "I'm not so sure. I've never made my own fun before. Why shouldn't I just drain you both right now?"

I fight the urge to run, and plant my feet firmly on the floor. "Because if you drain us we can't help you. Come on. Let's go back to Titotown and then, I promise, the fun will begin."

I hold my palms face up and concentrate on my dreambase. Soon a sparkling, gold portal forms and grows in the centre of our tree ring. Hesitantly the vampire steps through and we follow.

"I hope this works," Neena whispers.

"So do I," I reply. "I don't really fancy being Vlad the Inhaler's dinner."

Then I cross my fingers and step through the portal back into Titotown.

CHAPTER EIGHT
TEACHING AN OLD VAMPIRE NEW TRICKS

Since I became a Dreamweaver, a lot of things I once thought impossible have become the opposite. For example, I had never imagined myself having a playdate with a vampire, but here I am, doing just that.

For our plan to work, Neena and I have to combine our dreamweaving powers. Standing back-to-back, we concentrate on weaving as many different fun activities as possible.

I weave a skate ramp along with some rollerblades, a BMX, a whole array of different sports items and even a trampoline! Without Neena, making that many items would take me an entire night's sleep, but with Neena lending me her powers it flows easily – like turning on a tap. As always, I'm in awe. Neena is incredibly powerful, more than she realizes.

I turn around to see what she's created and burst out laughing. There's a giant inflatable bouncy castle on my clifftop! She's also made an art station, loads of different videogames and an orchestra's worth of instruments.

The vampire looks at it all with an open mouth, and claps its hands together in glee. "Oh, I can't wait for someone to use all of this so I can *suck* the fun right out of them!" it cheers merrily.

I try not to facepalm. "No, *you're* going to be having the fun, remember?" I encourage the creature. "Come on, why don't we try the skate ramp first."

And now somehow, I, Tito, am teaching
a Vampire how to skateboard. I hold on to
its horribly dry and bony hand as it wobbles
about, making strange little "Ooooh" and
"Eeeek" noises.

"I'm not sure about this one," Neena
whispers in my ear. "Why don't we try some
of the other activities?"

We walk the vampire through painting
(it paints an entirely black canvas) and then

knitting, which isn't so easy with its spindly fingers. Then we try a racing game on one of the consoles. It seems to like that one; I even see it smiling at one point. Neena lets the vampire win and it jumps up and down – giving me a high five.

"Yes, yes, my little pixel car thwarted yours!" it sings out and I can't help but laugh along. Am I actually having *fun*?

But more importantly, it looks like our vampire is having fun too. It runs over to the collection of instruments and picks up the biggest, heaviest horn, the kind you have to wear to play.

"Tito, have you noticed it looks different now? Kind of … healthier and happier?" Neena whispers to me.

I look at the vampire, happily honking on the tuba, and notice a rosy colour in its cheeks. It *does* look better. The vampire hobbles over to us, still wearing the tuba, and blows loudly.

"Oh, listen to that sound!" it says, beaming with its tiny mouth. "Children, I must thank you. I haven't felt this full … well, ever. I truly am having my own fun."

"That's amazing." Neena smiles. "So … you won't be feeding on funergy any more?"

The vampire chuckles a little shyly. "No, no. I shall return to the spirit world and inform my vampire brethren that we may feed ourselves forevermore! Perhaps we need not be solitary hunters after all."

"Well, fun *is* better shared," I agree.

The vampire thanks us once again and then disappears in a cloud of white mist, taking the tuba with it.

Neena and I turn to each other silently, pause and then erupt into cheers. We jump up and down, whooping and hugging.

"We did it!" I say, finally collapsing on the floor.

Neena joins me and we look out at Titotown. Everything in my dreambase still seems fuzzy and strange. Even the items we just dreamweaved for the vampire are now beginning to twist and change shape.

"I have a feeling," Neena says quietly, "that even though the vampire's gone, something's still wrong."

"He said he didn't know who the Bhoot was, though. Do you think your uncle *is* involved somehow?"

Neena points to the portal at the edge of the cliff, the one we jumped through from the Everwood clifftop. It's even larger now.

"That portal doesn't look like a mistake. Someone has made that on purpose – a portal from your dreambase to the human world. Plus, what the vampire said about a grid…" Neena shakes her head. "I feel like there's more for us to uncover."

"We will," I say confidently, even though my tummy feels a bit wobbly. "Maybe Grandad can help us— Oh no, Grandad!"

We both jump to our feet. In all the vampire craziness, I'd forgotten we left Grandad sitting on the cliff in the waking world, completely drained!

Neena and I hurry to the large portal. She jumps through before me and I follow after, trying not to look down as my feet step off the edge of the cliff.

The next thing I know, I'm waking up on the cold, wet grass on Everwood clifftop with drizzle that makes me shiver. I hear Neena groan and I open my eyes. We're lying under a red raincoat that has a familiar musky scent…

"Welcome back to the land of the waking," Grandad says, smiling down at us. He's in his blue shirt and I realize it's his jacket covering us.

"Grandad!"

I jump up and wrap my arms around him.

"Are you OK?" Neena joins in the hug and Grandad squeezes us both back. "I'm just fine! That fun fiend nearly inhaled all the joy out of me again and I would have been a boring zombie person but luckily the fairies helped me out."

I look around and see a few of the sparkling fairies hiding up in the tree branches, giggling. The fairies are *officially* back in my good books!

"Now let's get you home. You're both

soaked and I don't want you catching colds. You can fill me in on the way."

"And I should probably ring my mum and let her know what's going on," Neena says, getting out her phone.

That's going to be a looooong call…

★

When we arrive home, everyone is still dull as a doornail. Mum and Mama are watching a chess tournament on TV and Nan is just staring at the wall. Even Roberto is napping – something that's usually impossible to get him to do!

"Give them some time," Grandad says gently. "They probably need to learn how to have fun again."

He digs out some chocolate ice creams from the very back of the freezer for me and Neena, before going to try to tempt the rest of the family with them.

Neena and I go to our room to eat our ice creams and discuss our next moves. As we sit down on our camp-beds, I feel a heaviness come over me.

"What's wrong, Tito?" Neena says, looking at my face carefully.

"I'm fine," I say, but I can't supress my deep sigh.

Neena raises her eyebrow at me. "I can tell when something is making you sad – your lip wobbles."

I lick my ice cream sadly and sigh again. "It's just … this was supposed to be a fun holiday for you. Your first time visiting the seaside! And it's been a disaster."

Surprisingly Neena starts giggling.

"What is it?" I'm very confused now.

"Oh, Tito. We just chased a vampire through like *seven* different dreambases from across the world, taught it to play the tuba AND we have chocolate ice cream.

Of course I'm having fun!"

I giggle a little too. The heaviness isn't so bad any more.

"Anyway, we don't have to do anything special. I just like being your friend." Neena shrugs. "We're a dream team, remember? Speaking of which, I've been thinking about this grid."

"Me too!" I blurt. "Sorry, you go first."

Neena finishes off the last of her ice cream and claps her hands together. "So you know all the dreams we were hopping through when we were chasing the vampire?" she says, her green eyes burning into mine. "What if they were dreambases of other Dreamweavers? After all, the vampire said that the power in the 'grid' was making dreambases easier to break in to."

I nod along, taking it in. "I was thinking the same thing! And the dreambases we saw, some of them were very famous locations...

Wait, I've got an idea."

Behind me is Grandad's desk where he keeps his computer but also his books, in the shelves above and drawers below. I rummage inside one of the larger drawers and find what I'm looking for – a large, flat book titled *World Atlas*. Then I grab a pencil and ruler from the desk.

"The first place we landed was here, the Pyramids," I explain, drawing a dot on Egypt. "Then the rainforest, then that temple place… it looked so familiar. Neena, google 'big square temple South America'."

Neena types quickly on her phone and then we scroll through the image results. "This one!"

I put another dot on Yucatán, Mexico.

"And, Tito, look, a news article about strange sightings around the temple this past week." Neena reads the online article, her eyes scanning the page wildly. "Locals are saying it's the Mayan gods, but lots of these sound like jinn sightings to me."

We work through the other sites we recognized in the dreams: the Eiffel Tower, Stonehenge, even Everwood clifftop and the high school.

As we go, Neena finds more and more news articles and social media posts about surges of unusual activity – glowing circular lights and strange creatures appearing – all within the last week.

When we're finished, the world map has lots of little pencil dots on it – I hope that Grandad doesn't mind me writing in his book, but I think he'll understand. Dreamweaving detective work is important!

"OK, here's what I'm thinking," I explain, grabbing the ruler. "What if…"

I draw a line from one of the dots straight to another.

"All these dreambases…"

I draw another line that connects three dots.

"Are linked together…"

I draw another line through the remaining dots, and then another.

"On the same lines … like—"

"A grid!" Neena beams.

Once I've drawn lines through all the spots, a clear criss-cross grid emerges with parallel lines that run kind of diagonally across the page.

"And these aren't even all the dreambases, only the ones we know," Neena babbles excitedly. "I bet they would form a massive grid all the way across the world. Like those power lines that carry electricity! Only these lines carry dream magic."

I sit back and stare at the page. A magical power grid that covers the world...

"And the vampire said the power grid has more power surging through it than usual," I think aloud. "Which is why Titotown is all messed up and creating those little squashed portals through to Everwood clifftop. And why the vampire found it so easy to jump through to all those dreambases when we were chasing him. The alliance's goal has always been to break down the barriers between the spirit world and the human world. They must be behind this extra dream magic flooding the grid."

Neena shudders. "We have to stop them."

"Neena! Tito! Dinner time," Grandad calls from the kitchen.

"We will fix it, but I think we've done enough for today," I say, rubbing my neck. I suddenly feel very tired – I guess sleeping on a clifftop while chasing a vampire will do that.

"You're right," Neena agrees with a yawn. "The vampire is gone, so tomorrow Everwood and everyone in it should be back to their usual fun selves. Then we can ask your grandad to help us fix the power grid. Let's deal with one thing at a time."

"And to be safe, I don't think we should dreamweave tonight," I add.

When you don't draw your symbol on your hand before going to sleep, you won't go to your home base. After dreamweaving almost every night, it feels weird closing my eyes, then *nothing,* before opening them again in the morning.

"Most importantly…" I say.

"What is it?" Neena asks nervously.

"We should stay off-grid." I wink, ignoring Neena's groans.

Badly timed jokes are my speciality.

CHAPTER NINE
HIDE OR FIGHT?

When my eyelids flutter open the next morning, it takes a while for my vision to adjust. Everything looks *different* somehow. I sit up and rub my eyes with the backs of my hands, letting them refocus. But the scene stays the same.

The whole room has no colour! Every single thing in it is grey and white, including…

"Argh!" I cry out, looking properly at my hands. They are a sad grey colour instead of peachy pink.

"What?" Neena groans, turning over on her camp-bed. "Oh!" She springs upright and looks around the room frantically.

I feel panic rising in my chest and rush over to the window, pulling back the white curtains that used to be dark red.

"Everything outside is grey and white too!" I exclaim, breathing heavily. Neena runs to join me and we stare at the newspaper-print world.

"But that must mean…" Neena turns and rushes from the bedroom. I follow close behind, knowing exactly what she's worried about.

Sure enough we find Mum, Mama and Nan, all in grey and white, sitting side by side on the flowery sofa concentrating on sudokus. I run up to Mama and click my fingers in front of her face, but she doesn't even look up from the puzzle.

"Tito, there's bran flakes in the kitchen

for breakfast," she says in a monotone.

"And tap water to mix them with," Mum adds, writing a 'zero' in one of her boxes.

I shudder at the sight of my parents, who are usually so bouncy in the morning, sitting quietly on the sofa. I shudder even harder at the thought of bran flakes for breakfast. Neena is waving her hand in front of Nan's face but she simply sighs heavily and continues concentrating on her puzzle book.

"I don't understand," Neena whispers to me. "The vampire said it would stop draining humans, but they're even worse today!"

"It said it was going back to the spirit world. Maybe it lied to us," I wonder out loud. "I really believed it had changed its ways, though."

I chew my lip as I look at grey-and-white Neena in front of me. It's so strange that I almost feel like I'm dreaming, but unfortunately I'm horribly awake.

Suddenly a jolt of panic runs through me. "Where's Roberto?"

We look around the room for my baby brother but there's no sign of Roberto or Grandad.

"Maybe he's still in bed?" Neena says, worry glinting in her eyes. Usually Roberto is the first one up, yelling and poking everyone until they get up too.

We go to check on him and sure enough,

Roberto is still asleep in his cot. He must be so bored that all he wants to do is sleep. Grandad is there too, staring down at my brother, a confused look on his face.

"Grandad, are you OK?" I ask, putting a hand on his back.

He shakes his head as if he's trying to dislodge a memory in there.

"I'm not sure," he says. "I have this feeling that yesterday … something was different."

"Yes," Neena urges. "It was! Try to remember. There was a vampire that was draining your fun but then the fairies helped you get back to normal."

"Ahhh yes, the fairies…" Grandad is really struggling, and he sits down on the bed. "I think I'll just have a little lie-down and look at the ceiling while I think about it."

I pull a blanket over Grandad. Then I put a few of Roberto's toys next to him in his cot, hoping it might spark some fun when he wakes up. This is wrong. It's all wrong!

I turn to Neena with a burning feeling in my chest. "I know we wanted Grandad to help us fix the grid but there's no time to get him back to normal. We have to go back to Everwood clifftop ourselves and make sure the vampire kept its promise. We'll find a way to fix the power grid when we're there."

"You're right," says Neena. "We can do this. It's always been just us before, so we can do it again now. Dream Team!"

A smile forms on my lips. "Dream Team."

★

Walking along Everwood high street in grey and white feels like walking in the pages of a book, or one of those old movies that Nan likes to watch. But even stranger are the woods, whose usual dark rich greens are now the colour of soot and ash. If Neena weren't beside me, I don't know if I'd have the courage to venture into the trees and climb the hill. I've definitely gotten braver since becoming a Dreamweaver, but I think *anyone* would get the heebie-jeebies walking into thick, colourless woods.

"Can you feel that?" Neena says in a hushed tone, as we reach the top of the hill. "It's like electricity in the air."

The hairs on my arms prick up – I do feel it. It's like a buzzing in the airwaves that gets stronger the closer we get to the clifftop. The sensation is similar to what I feel when I'm dreamweaving. It's like a power that starts in your fingertips then flows out of your hands in waves.

"Is it … dream magic?" I ask.

When we finally emerge into the clearing on the Everwood clifftop, it's obvious what's causing the buzzing feeling.

All the tiny misshapen portals that were here before have disappeared. Instead, the

portal at the edge of the cliff is now a vast,
swirling vortex, with jagged edges and a
burning light. A burning *green* light. Against
the grey-and-white world around it, the
colour is horrifically luminous. The wind
tunnel created by the portal is picking up
leaves and twigs
nearby and
sucking them
in like a black
hole.

"Green,"
I breathe.
"It's definitely
the Bhoot."

"Tito, you
don't have to do
this," Neena says
suddenly. "He's my
uncle. We still don't know
how to fix the power grid and I'm pretty sure

the only way we can find out is by going into that portal. It's going to be dangerous."

My stomach flips and every cell in my body is urging me to turn back. But my heart knows what to do.

"Listen, if you're jumping into a giant green portal, then *I'm* jumping into a giant green portal too," I say, holding my chin up. "Let's do this!"

Neena laughs a little and then pauses. "I'm a bit scared. You're so good at facing your fears. How do you do it?"

I think for a moment. "Sometimes when you feel scared, you have to block out the voices in your head and just push through. Like this – AARRRRRGH!" I yell, holding my hands out wide.

"Got it." Neena grins, holding my hand. "Together? Three … two … one!"

We both run at full pelt towards the portal and scream at the top of our lungs.

"AAAAAAAAAAAAAAARRRRRR-GGGGGGGHHHHHHHHHHHHHH!"

As we get closer, the vortex picks us up and sucks us in, spinning us around like we're on a roller coaster. I'm so dizzy I feel like my head might fly off, then we're suddenly spat out into my dreambase, leaving our sleeping bodies in the human world.

We both land – *oof* – on our backs in the grass. The sky above us is a dark midnight blue. "Sweet, sweet colours." I sigh, holding my spinning head. "I never thought I'd be so happy to see blue."

But as the dizziness wears off, I take a look at the rest of Titotown and things are even worse than before. Everything is warped and blurred, like a canvas that's had water thrown on it, making the paint drip and run. The colours bleed into each other and it's hard to see where the trees start and the clifftop ends.

"Well, the vampire isn't here," Neena says,

squinting at the wacky world around us.
"But I think you're right that the Bhoot
and the alliance know about the power grid.
They must be the ones making it like *this*."

All of a sudden, from some far-off place, a
voice floats through the air. A familiar voice.
"Children! Children! Help me…"

Neena and I look around frantically but
there's no one else here apart from us.

"That's the vampire's voice," Neena gasps.

"Tito… Neena…" the vampire calls again, its voice echoey. "I'm stuck in Neena's dream… Please help!"

A shiver runs down my spine and I feel cold all over. "Neena, why do I feel like this is *definitely* a trap?" I say slowly.

But Neena's eyes are wide with fear. "Listen to its voice! It really sounds like it's in trouble. The vampire needs our help."

"I have a really bad feeling about this," I urge. "I don't think we should travel to your dreambase. The alliance is already messing with the power grid and we don't have a plan to fix it yet. *And* we know the Bhoot needs your powers for his plan to work. We have to keep you safe!"

"But as long as we're in my dreambase we'll be fine," Neena counters. "The Bhoot doesn't have my symbol, I've kept it so secret. Only you know it."

To enter the dream of a Dreamweaver you *have* to know their symbol and draw it on your hand before sleeping, so I guess Neena has a point.

I know there's no talking Neena out of this – she wants to help the vampire and I want to help her. So, even though everything in me wants to cover Neena in bubble wrap and take her back home, I have to go with her.

As Neena starts to create a sparkling portal to her home base, I have a realization – sometimes protecting someone means fighting alongside them, not hiding them away. I sigh.

"Bring it on."

CHAPTER TEN
TRAPPED AND TRICKED!

My legs shake as we enter the golden portal leading to Neena's dreambase. I close my eyes as we step in and am suspended in the darkness before shooting out the other side.

I almost don't want to open my eyes for fear of what we'll find. But when I hear Neena gasp next to me, I know that I have to.

"No!" I cry out, stumbling backwards.

"Hello, Neena," snarls the Bhoot in his sickeningly smooth voice. "And you brought your friend too, how sweet."

He is standing, tall and thin, in his sharp-cut tunic top with long sleeves. A flat hat sits atop his head with one long feather at the front. Neena's dreambase of Chitral valley stretches out behind him. It's usually so beautiful but now seems vast and empty.

Five other people stand beside him. I shudder as I take in the alliance – a group of Soothsayers that have joined the Bhoot. Two men and two women, dressed all in dark colours, glare at us menacingly. A few smile, but it's not at all friendly. I'm surprised to see that one of the members is quite young – a teenage boy.

"Tito, look," Neena breathes, holding tightly on to my arm.

I follow her gaze to just behind the group, where a large iron crate stands, its bars thick and glowing green. Inside, a small pale figure trembles – it's the vampire! It does need our help after all.

"Ah, children, you came!" it cheers in a wobbly voice. "I'm so sorry, I really did want to stop draining your world of fun, but the alliance captured me just after I left you last night. They forced me to return to Everwood and suck every last drop of fun from it. I didn't want to, I promise. Please help me escape!"

I feel a pang of guilt for thinking the vampire had lied to us.

I *also* feel a pang of annoyance that Neena didn't listen to me. I knew this was a bad idea! But now's not the time for me to stick my tongue out and sing "*I told you sooooo*".

"How did you enter my dream, Uncle?" Neena shouts, her voice shaking with anger.

The Bhoot simply laughs and gestures to a short, squat woman beside him.

"This will be news to you," she says in a shrill voice. "But through multiple star readings I deduced that all dreambases are connected by a power grid, fuelled by dream magic."

So this woman is a Darkreader, she can read the stars like Neena's mum. Only Ameena uses *her* powers for good not evil. I scoff and immediately regret it. The Bhoot glares at me with his bright green eyes.

"Sorry, it's just we'd already worked that out." I shrug.

"I find that hard to believe," the Darkreader snaps. "Anyway, we realized that flooding multiple dreambases with our powers would cause the grid to break down. We have three of the most powerful Darkweavers in our alliance, so it didn't take too long."

A man with a pointed black beard nods, along with a smaller old woman with shiny silver hair tied into a bun. These two must be the other Darkweavers in the group. From some detective work Neena and I did a few weeks ago, I know they are Namira Sylvester and Seeyah Khan. Their nicknames are the Silver Cat and the Night King.

"Once the power grid was corrupted, the barriers between our world and the dream realm broke down," the Bhoot takes over, smirking. "We don't need symbols any more, we can simply step through into any dream we desire. I know your dreambase is this valley in Chitral, my dear Neena, so I simply stepped through from the human world. All of us Soothsayers can – not just Dreamweavers."

This is worse than we thought! Not only are worlds starting to merge, but the alliance has access to anyone's dreams they want.

"You are *Dark*weavers, not *Dream*weavers," Neena shouts. "You don't get to call yourself that."

The Bhoot glides towards us and we shrink back. "Really, Neena, what's dark and light, good and bad? Don't you think it's wrong that us Soothsayers have to hide ourselves away from normal humans, for fear they will cast us out. Like *you* were cast out of Chitral?"

"I was cast out because of *you*," Neena retorts, tears in her eyes. "Because everyone thought I'd end up evil like you."

The Bhoot freezes. "I am not evil, Neena. I simply want what's best for us Soothsayers. Once the spirit world and the human world become one, with no dream realm in the way, the jinn can help *us* become rulers of the world!"

My body goes cold with shock as I hear

what the Bhoot is saying. Taking over the world? This is *way* bigger than a few scary fairies or a hangry wolf. My heart starts to beat wildly.

"The jinn will never agree to it," Neena says, shaking her head. "How will you convince them?"

The Bhoot turns towards a muscular man with the biggest biceps I've ever seen. They look like watermelons on each arm. "Like this," he says, clicking his fingers.

The muscly man walks over to the vampire's cage, lifts his hands and closes his eyes.

"Let me out, you fiend!" the vampire cries.

But the man is chanting words in a language I've never heard before. Sparkling black waves travel from his hands towards the cage where the vampire bangs on the bars.

Immediately, the vampire drops its hands, smiles and turns to the Bhoot, bowing deeply.

"Master," it says in a flat voice.

"A Darkcaster," Neena gasps. "They're going to put all the jinn under a spell."

"Now, Neena," the Bhoot says, coming ever closer. "Enough is enough. It is time for you to join us and take your place as the sixth and final member of the alliance. Do not deny your immense power any longer. You are the strongest Dreamweaver I've ever taught—"

The Night King coughs.

"OK, *one* of the strongest Dreamweavers…"

The man smiles, seemingly happy with this. I roll my eyes.

"And we need you, Neena."

"Never!" she says, stamping her foot and balling up her fists.

"Very well, we'll do this the hard way," the Bhoot says.

He grits his teeth and a neon-green glow starts to surround him. But before he can

attack, Neena thrusts her hands forward
shooting a beam of pure golden dream energy
at her uncle.

In one leap, the Bhoot flies into the air,
dodging the blast and aiming his own right
back at us!

Neena and I jump apart as the blast hits the
earth between us, leaving a scorch mark.

I end up further towards the riverbank and Neena is over to my right, crouched by some shrubbery. We've been separated!

Floating about three metres in the air, I see the Bhoot's head snap around in my direction and he fixes me in his glare. His hands start glowing green and a smile spreads across his face as he plans his next blast … aimed right at me!

I throw my hands up to shield myself just as he strikes.

"Tito, NO!" Neena yells.

A massive flash of bright light engulfs me, and I hear a clanging sound as heat surrounds my body. When I open my eyes, Neena has dreamweaved a huge, round golden shield in front of me and it's protecting me from the blast!

The Bhoot maintains his ray of green focused energy and Neena's shield stays put, but now the other Darkweavers are adding

their powers to boost the Bhoot's attack.

I look over at Neena who is straining, her legs bracing against the ground in a deep lunge as she puts all her strength into protecting me. I know I have to help her so I dig deep, hold up my hands and add my own dream magic to the shield. It grows even larger and brighter, the combined light and power of our dream magic lighting up the whole valley like a fireworks display. Our shield is glowing brighter and stronger than the Bhoot's magic now, and it's all down to Neena's power.

We're going to win! We're going to beat him!

"Yes!" the Bhoot cackles wildly and my heart stops.

Why is he laughing?

A deafening cracking sound rips through the sky.

Neena and I glance at each other in concern, while still trying to maintain the shield.

Another crack rings out, then another, until suddenly the whole sky above the valley shatters into pieces like a stained-glass window.

Immediately the Bhoot and the Darkweavers drop their attack and Neena collapses, exhausted from the amount of magic she's used.

"Neena!" I cry out, dropping down beside her. The Bhoot chuckles menacingly and floats back down to the ground, his tunic flapping in the breeze.

I know in my gut that we've been tricked, and I'm terrified to think about what we might have unleashed.

"Children…" The Bhoot smiles at us. "It is done."

CHAPTER ELEVEN
TITO TO THE RESCUE

"Come on, Neena, we have to go now!"
I tug on Neena's arm, begging her to get
up, but she groans weakly.

The shattered sky starts to bleed colour
down on to the valley and portals are opening
up all around me.

There are fairies, a halmasti and other jinn
I've never seen before emerging from them.
The merging worlds are causing the dream
realm to go into chaos.

The halmasti – large, wolfy and dark red
– comes bounding up to us. I shrink away

in fear before I realize who the sharp teeth belong to.

"Hal!" I cry out in relief.

"Tito, Neena! What's going on?" he replies, looking alarmed.

The last time we met, Neena and I stopped Hal's hangry rampage through our head teacher's dreams and helped him return to Chitral. The alliance had been using him too.

"The Bhoot forced us to create a massive power surge here in Neena's dreambase and now the grid has broken down completely. The spirit world, human world and dream realm are merging into one!"

Hal's slanted eyes shine with anger and he turns to where the alliance members are gathering in a circle with the Bhoot in the middle, issuing instructions.

"They're going to cast spells on all the jinn to turn you into his army. You need to get out of here," I urge.

"But what about you two?" Hal says, looking down at Neena with concern. "Can she run?"

"Leave me," Neena splutters out. "Save yourself."

"Are you bonkers?" I gawp. "No way!"

"Capture all the jinn," the Bhoot booms loudly and his voice echoes across the valley. "We must get to work."

"What about your niece and her friend?" the teenage boy says. He's been silent up until now, watching everything going on with narrowed eyes.

"We have no use for her any more," the Bhoot says waving his hand. "But I suppose you could capture them, just in case."

Hal growls and turns to me, lowering his hulking body. "Get on!" he instructs.

I don't even think about it. Hal and I help Neena on to his back and I follow, grabbing his thick, matted fur and clambering up. I circle my arms around her and then hold tightly on to Hal's neck so we don't fall off. I've always wanted to learn how to ride a horse – I suppose a giant wolf is a good place to start.

The Silver Cat is advancing towards us now, flanked by the Night King who is rubbing his hands together with glee.

"Let's go!" I yell.

Hal rears up on his hind legs, howls and pounces into a full sprint.

"Get back here!" I hear the Silver Cat shout from behind us.

"*No chance!*" I call back.

"Where are we headed?" Hal huffs, running as hard as he can.

"Uh… Um…" I scan the terrain around us frantically as Hal careens across the valley. We need to find a way out, back to Everwood, but everything in Neena's dreambase has become so warped, I can't figure out where I am. If I could just have a moment to collect myself then I could create a portal to escape, but we can't stop or the alliance will catch us.

I feel tears brim in my eyes but I blink them away. *How will I get us out?*

"Tito? Titooooo…" a familiar voice calls out on the breeze.

My heart leaps. "Grandad?" I shout.

"Tito! Focus on my voice. I'm on Everwood clifftop with yours and Neena's sleeping bodies. Make a portal back to me."

I look back and see the Bhoot high in the air, flying after us on a cloud of green smoke.

"I don't think I can!" I call back.

"You can do it, Tito. Be brave!" Grandad replies.

Taking a deep breath, I think about what Neena has taught me – that only those who feel emotions deeply have the gift of dreamweaving. Right now, the only thing

I feel deeply is terrified! But when I look
down at Neena crumpled against Hal's back
I find something even stronger – the urge to
save my friend.

"Just focus on my voice," Grandad says, and
his voice sounds like it's coming from my left.

"Hal, I'm going to create a portal to my
dreambase," I say, my voice shaking with
the force of his legs pounding the ground.
"When I say so, I need you to take a sharp
left."

"Roger that!" Hal replies.

I close my eyes and concentrate, focusing on Titotown in my mind. I feel a tingling sensation fill my body and when I open my eyes, I sense golden sparks to my left-hand side.

"NOW!" I shout out.

Hal lurches to the left, his back paws sliding against the grass.

"I did it!" I yell, beaming.

A golden portal has appeared before us!

"Go through without me," Hal shouts. "I need to stay behind to warn the other jinn."

"But Hal, I – *whhhhhaaaoooo!*"

Hal bucks forward on his front legs, catapulting us off his back and into the portal.

We're suspended in the nothingness and then crash-land into Titotown near the pine-tree forest, which is now just a collection of squiggly green shapes and jagged portals.

I quickly turn and close the portal behind me by swirling my hands anticlockwise.

The Bhoot may be able to access my dreambase easily now, but that should slow him down. What we really need is to return to the human world.

"I can sense you're closer." Grandad's voice floats through the air. "Now come back to Everwood clifftop, you're nearly there."

"Tito?" Neena says weakly, lying beside me on the grass.

"Neena, we're almost home, can you walk?" I ask.

Neena tries to push herself up from the floor but collapses again.

My mind races. The Bhoot wasn't far behind us. If he's still chasing us, it won't be long until he's here. I have to protect Neena and that means getting us out of here, but she's still too weak to move! Suddenly my mind flashes back to Mama pushing Roberto along the promenade in his pushchair. *That's it.*

As quickly as I can I raise my hands and weave a large pushchair with reinforced wheels. It kind of looks like a pushchair crossed with a monster truck but I don't care, it'll do. I heave Neena up and flop her into the makeshift vehicle. The ground under my feet starts to feel soggy and sticky as my dreambase disintegrates around us.

I start pushing but the wheels keep getting stuck in the earth. I suddenly feel very sorry for my parents having to push me and now Roberto around – pushchairs are tricky! Luckily I manage to gain some momentum and the pushchair starts moving.

The large green portal that the Bhoot
created through to Everwood clifftop is
still open and glowing brightly. I head
towards it, gritting my teeth with the effort
of pushing Neena through the sinking floor.

"Nearly ... there," I grunt, panting heavily.

With one last giant heave, I shove the
pushchair and Neena through the portal.
Then, taking a last look at my broken
Titotown, I step through after her.

We wake up, cold and soggy on the wet
floor of Everwood clifftop.

Grandad is looking down at me, his eyes
shining with fear. "Tito, Neena. I finally
came to my senses at home and you were
gone. I guessed you'd be here trying to fix
things. What on earth happened?"

Neena replies before I can say anything.
"Tito saved me."

CHAPTER TWELVE
A NEW WORLD

"I can't believe I let the Bhoot trick me,"
Neena fumes, kicking the ground angrily.

We're hurrying back down the hill and
I've just finished explaining what happened
to Grandad.

Neena is in full-blown rage mode.
She picks up a rock and hurls it as hard
as she can down the slope. Well, at least
she's got her strength back. "How could
I have been so stupid?" she mutters.

"You were protecting me with that shield,"
I point out. "You had no other choice but to

use your dream magic. We can't have known that would be the last straw for the power grid."

"So the human world and spirit world are merging completely?" Grandad says, a far-off look in his eye. "Well, that does explain things."

I look at him sideways. "What do you mean?"

Grandad sighs. "There's good news and bad news. You're about to see for yourself."

We're at the bottom of the hill now, and the sensation of electricity buzzing in the air is even stronger than before. It makes me feel a bit light-headed.

"A little while after you left, I felt the fun returning to my body. As you can see, the colour has returned to the world and people are slowly getting back to normal, which must be happening because the vampire is in that cage. But the bad news is..."

Grandad says heavily. "*This* has happened."

We turn on to Everwood high street and my first feeling is relief. There's colour, the shops are open and there are people walking around.

But that's not all.

Large, swirling portals in dark purple, midnight blue and gold are stretching open around us – across the main road, above the roof of the butcher's, even swallowing up

half of a bus stop. Inside them, strange and unfamiliar buildings start to appear, with roads leading off deeper into the portals.

"The spirit world," Neena breathes. "So that's what it looks like…"

Out of the portals, figures are slowly emerging, looking around at Everwood with confused expressions. Jinn. I look up and see two moons sitting brightly against a pink sky. An elf crosses the street in front of me.

I turn to Neena in shock. "OK, am I still dreaming or is this really happening?"

"I'm afraid you are wide awake," Grandad answers sadly.

Neena stares back at me with her green eyes wide. "The worlds have merged."

I observe the people on the streets around us. Surely they must be freaking out too? But although some of them point and stare, and I spot a few people even disappearing into their houses and shutting the doors, they seem quite calm. Actually, not calm, *tired*.

A lady pushing a pram is leaning on it to keep herself upright and yawning loudly. Another old man on a bench is fully asleep – snoring loudly and dribbling on his chin.

"I think the dream magic is too strong for them," Neena says, looking at the dark circles under the eyes of people around us. "It's making them fall asleep!"

We continue to walk back to Nan and

Grandad's house, watching as the world we know shifts and morphs in front of our eyes into a new world – one with jinn, strange landscapes and portals.

When we're nearly home Neena gets a call from her mum who speaks rapidly down the phone. Grandad and I leave her in the driveway and go inside.

"Mum, Mama, I'm home!" I call. I'm excited to see my parents after they've been zombie versions of themselves for so long. And after my showdown with the Bhoot!

But there's no answer.

"Check the living room," Grandad suggests, so I go through, and that's where I find them.

Nan, Mama and Mum are curled up on the sofa together, fast asleep! They've pulled Nan's handmade quilted blanket over them and all three are snoring loudly. Only Roberto is alert and awake, bashing puzzle pieces around on the floor.

"Berto!" I cheer, beaming.

I scoop him up, making him squeal with delight. I'm so happy to see my baby brother back to normal, I don't notice Neena coming in behind me, her face pale.

"What is it, sweetheart?" Grandad asks, making me turn around.

"Mum says the same thing has happened back home," Neena explains. "The worlds have merged *everywhere*, and *everyone* is falling asleep, apart from Soothsayers it seems."

166

"If it's only Soothsayers that aren't affected by the dream magic," Grandad says, as he tickles Roberto under his chin, "then what's this one doing awake? Unless…" His eyes grow wide.

Neena and I nudge each other. "We had a feeling Berto might be a Dreamweaver too." I smile. "I guess this confirms it."

"Oh, wonderful!" Grandad says scooping up Roberto and bouncing him. "Two Dreamweavers in the family!"

I look at Mum, Mama and Nan zonked out on the sofa.

"But what are we going to do about them?" I sigh. "And the merged worlds? And the jinn army and the…"

I suddenly feel very overwhelmed and flop to the floor, my head in my hands. Neena sits beside me and puts her arm around my shoulders.

"I have an idea but you might not like it,"

she says quietly. "If we're going to fight the Bhoot and fix the power grid, we're going to need reinforcements. And there's only one place we can go to do that."

I turn to look at Neena slowly, reality sinking in at what she's suggesting.

"Jinn *do* know the most about the power grid," I say, nodding slowly. "If anyone knows how to fix it, it will be them. And we have to warn them about the Bhoot's plan. So I guess that means..."

Neena nods back at me, her expression serious. "It's time for *us* to travel to the spirit world."

"Has ... anyone ever done that before?" I gulp.

Neena shakes her head.

I let that sink in. I'll be going somewhere that no Dreamweaver, no *human*, has gone before.

And I need to do it to wake up the world.

To fix the power grid. And to stop the alliance. A strange calm comes over me as I look at my best friend. Together, we've achieved things I'd never have dreamed of in a million years: freeing fairies, befriending wolves, saving vampires…

"If anyone's going to be the first," I say, "it's got to be us."

Neena smiles and her eyes blaze fiercely. "Let's save the world?" she says, holding out her hand.

I shake it. "Let's do it."

JOIN THE DREAM TEAM IN
THEIR NEXT ADVENTURE...

DREAM
WEAVERS

QUEST TO SAVE THE
SPIRIT WORLD

COMING 2025!

ABOUT THE AUTHOR

Annabelle Sami is a writer and arts producer living in London. She writes diverse mystery stories and 'anarchically silly fun' (*Guardian*) comedy books for children. Her book *Llama Out Loud* was shortlisted for the Waterstones Children's Book Prize, who wrote, 'Sami constructs her story with flawless comic timing' and won the Spark! Book Award 2020. Annabelle's mission in all her work is to give funny, smart and adventurous children of colour characters they can relate to.

ABOUT THE ILLUSTRATOR

Forrest Burdett is an illustrator
from New Jersey with an eye for whimsy,
a heart full of magic, and a passion for
vibrant colours. He studied Illustration
at the Fashion Institute of Technology
and now lives in Portland, Oregon.
He loves finding magic in the small,
everyday moments and uses his art as
a means to explore and share them.
You can find more of his work at
forrestburdett.com